Charles M. Schulz

You're Our New Mascot, Chuck!

 HarperCollins®

Copyright © 1998 United Feature Syndicate, Inc. PEANUTS © United Feature Syndicate, Inc.
Based on the PEANUTS® comic strip by Charles M. Schulz. Printed and bound in China. All rights reserved.

"The meeting of the board of the Pelicans baseball team will come to order! Today we're going to vote on whether or not we call Chuck. I vote 'Yes'!"

"I vote 'No,'" said Marcie.

"I can't decide," said Franklin.

"Then the 'Yes' has it!"

"How come?"

"It was louder!"

"I shouldn't be telling you this Charles, but I feel I have to . . . Peppermint Patty is going to ask you to help her baseball team."

"She wants me to pitch?"

"Your optimism should be framed,
 Charles."

"Hey, Chuck, how would you like to help out my baseball team this year? We really need someone like you, Chuck . . ."

"But what about my own team? It would break their hearts if I left them."

"It would?"

"You did it, didn't you, Sir? You called Chuck and you told him that our team needs him!"

"Well,
we do,
Marcie."

"Yes, but he thinks
he's going to be
the pitcher or
linebacker or goalie
or something!"

"Peppermint Patty says her team needs me."

"Sure, like last year when she told you the same thing, and you ended up selling popcorn!"

"I forgot about that."

"You probably blockheaded it out of your mind!"

"Well, Chuck, I see you made it."

"I'm glad you asked me. Guess
you needed a good pitcher, huh?
Infielder? Outfielder? Catcher?
Am I getting close? What's left?"

"Oh, no!"

"Here's how it is, Chuck. All the big
league teams have mascots, right?
Our team is the Pelicans, right?
Well, we have this costume we want
you to wear. So try it on, Chuck,
and see what you think."

"Don't worry about it, Chuck, you look great! Flap your wings and dance around . . . act like a real pelican. The fans like lots of action!"

"Tomorrow's our first game, Chuck. I want you to go home and get a good rest. But don't take your costume off! I want you to think pelican and be pelican!"

"Charlie Brown? What's this about you being a mascot on Peppermint Patty's baseball team? I hear she's got you wearing a dumb pelican costume. What did you say? Why does your voice sound muffled?"

"It's hard to explain."

"Marcie! What are you doing here?"

"I want you to take off that stupid costume, Charles, and stop letting yourself be humiliated! If you won't do it for yourself, do it for someone who likes you."

"Kiss her, you blockhead!"

"Where's our pelican? The game's ready to start! Where's Chuck and the pelican costume?!"

"I told him he shouldn't come. I told him it was degrading."

"Marcie!"   "That's my name."

"Our pelican! He's here! Ha, Marcie, you were wrong! Chuck didn't listen to your stupid advice! He came anyway!"

"Take the head off, Chuck.
   I'm gonna give you a big kiss!"